Copyright © 1995 by NordSüd Verlag AG, CH-8005 Zürich, Switzerland.
First published in Switzerland under the title *Markus schimpft fürchterlich*.
English translation copyright © 1995 by North-South Books Inc., New York 10001.

First published in the United States, Great Britain, Canada, Australia, and New
Zealand in 1995 by North-South Books Inc., an imprint of NordSüd Verlag AG,
CH-8005 Zürich, Switzerland.
First paperback edition published in 1997.
Distributed in the United States by North-South Books Inc., New York 10001.

Library of Congress Cataloging-in-Publication Data
Lachner, Dorothea.
[Markus schimpft fürchterlich. English]
Andrew's angry words / Dorothea Lachner ; illustrated by Thé Tjong-Khing.
Summary: When his sister trips and sends all his toys flying, Andrew lets loose
a lot of nasty angry words that start to spread from person to person
creating trouble wherever they go.
[Anger—Fiction. 2. Behavior—Fiction.] I. Thé, Tjong-Khing, ill. II. Title.
PZ7.L1353An 1995 [E]—dc-20 94-40031

A CIP catalogue record for this book is available from The British Library.

ISBN 978-0-7358-2283-2 (trade binding)
5 7 9 TB 10 8 6
ISBN 1-55858-436-6 (library binding)
1 3 5 7 9 LB 10 8 6 4 2
ISBN 1-55858-769-4 (paperback)
7 9 PB 10 8 6
Printed in China by SNP Leefung Packaging & Printing (Dongguan) Co., Ltd.,
Dongguan, P.R.C., September 2009.

www.northsouth.com

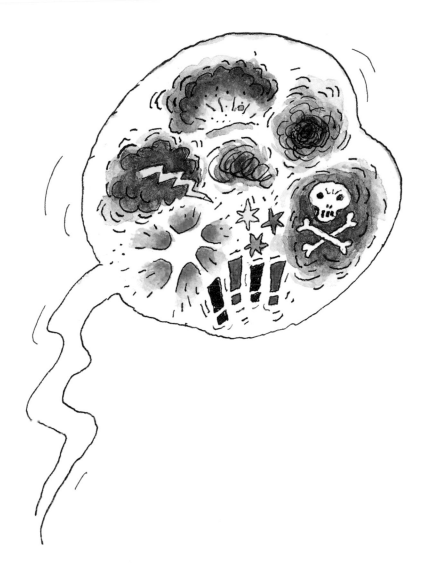

Dorothea Lachner

Andrew's ANGRY Words

Illustrated by Thé Tjong-Khing

NorthSouth
New York / London

When the phone rang, Marion yelled, "I'll get it!"
She ran through the living room, and she didn't see
her little brother until it was too late.

BAM! Andrew and all his books and toys went flying.

"Watch it!" yelled Andrew. And then he shouted
the ugliest bunch of angry words anyone has ever heard.
Right away Andrew wished he hadn't said them, but
it was too late. The angry words were out—passed along
to someone else.

Marion talked on the phone with Ted, the baker's son.

"I'm sorry, Marion," he said, "but I can't take you out for ice cream today. I have to work."

Marion was very disappointed; and before she knew it, she yelled all the angry words through the phone at Ted.

"This is terrible!" Andrew said to himself. "I've got to catch those words!" And he jumped up and ran around the corner to Ted's house.

But it was too late.

Ted was upset because Marion had been so angry with him. He jumped on his bike and rode off to work. But soon those angry words came rushing out from the bottom of his lungs and went flying right through an open window . . .

and into a room where a poet was deep in thought. When the angry words crashed in and interrupted his thoughts, he was furious. "Oh no! I've lost my rhyme!"

A few minutes later, just as his rhyme was coming back
to him, a motorcycle roared by and wiped it out of his head
again. So the poet leaned out of his window and screamed
those angry words at the man on the motorcycle.

The man on the motorcycle was late for work, so he took a shortcut.

But Princess Priscilla was taking her morning ride, and he had to slow down. At first he was annoyed . . . then he got impatient . . . and then he got so exasperated that the angry words came rushing out and hit the Princess in the back of the head.

Princess Priscilla rode along until a huge dragon blocked her path. He was very hungry and wanted a delicious horse for breakfast.

But the Princess refused to give up her horse. She scolded that dragon and shouted the angry words right up into his face. This made the dragon so angry that he lost his appetite and flew off in a huff.

Meanwhile, Andrew was still trying to catch up with the angry words. He had chased them from person to person and place to place, but he was always too late.

As Andrew flew through the clear blue sky, he saw the dragon, and he could tell that the dragon had the angry words.

But not for long.

Without his breakfast, the dragon was getting hungrier by the second, and the hunger was making him more and more angry. He flew over the bay and saw a fisherman with a basket of fresh fish. The dragon hated fish, but he was furious with the fisherman anyway because the fisherman had food while his own stomach was empty. So he roared those angry words at the fisherman.

When the fisherman got back to port, he went to the
market. The words the dragon had dumped on him were
still ringing in his ears, but he was trying to forget them.
Then a lady dropped a pumpkin right in front of him, and
he nearly tripped over it.

"Hey, watch out!" he yelled. "I could have hurt myself! Those things are dangerous! Why don't you be more careful?" And the fisherman stamped and shouted and spluttered until every last nasty, angry word lay there quivering on the ground.

"Stop being so dramatic,"
said the lady calmly. Then
she scooped up the angry
words, rolled them into
a ball,

shoved them into
an old potato sack,
tied the sack tightly,

and threw it into the ocean.

The sack twisted and jumped and bubbled and hissed, and the fish and crabs and starfish gathered around. The octopus got scared and sped away in a cloud of ink. But the sack soon lay still, and all the sea creatures went back about their business.

Back on shore, Andrew arrived at the market, all out of breath. The lady told him how she had put an end to the angry words.

"Thank you very much," said Andrew.

"It was nothing," said the lady. "Here is a present for you. These are all the kind and happy words I know. They're *nice* words. Hold on to them, and you'll fly all the way home."

As he flew over the sea, Andrew tossed some of the nice words to the fisherman . . .

and threw another little piece to the dragon, who was
so happy that he danced an elegant rumba in midair!

Andrew shared his gift with Princess Priscilla, who smiled a regal smile, stood up on her horse, and did a circus trick just for him.

When Andrew got back to town, the man on the
motorcycle stopped to let him cross the street. Andrew
gave him some nice words too. When the motorcycle sped
off, it went *Wuuuuoooommmmm*. But to Andrew it sounded
like *Thankyoouuummmm*!

Andrew waved as he flew past the poet.
"Here are some nice words," called Andrew. "I hope
you can use them!" The poet smiled and instantly began
to compose the happiest poem ever written.

And the boy at the bakery? When Andrew gave Ted
his share of the wonderful present, Ted decided to take
the afternoon off, just like that!

Ted stuffed his treasure in his pocket, raced home
on his bicycle, and phoned Marion.

"Hello, Marion? It's me, Ted. Would you still like to go
out for some ice cream?"

Marion felt a big warm smile coming through the phone
at her. And of course, she said, "Why, I'd love to!"

When Andrew got home, he told Marion all about his magic present.

"Look, Marion. I've broken off lots of pieces, and yet it's even bigger than it used to be! What shall I do with it?"

"I think you'd better keep it in a safe place," she said, "just in case those angry words ever come back. And Andrew? I'm sorry I knocked you over this morning."

So Andrew put the nice words into the
cupboard by his bed. That was a long time
ago, and the angry words still haven't
come back.